I saw a
BEE

ROB RAMSDEN

Scallywag Press Ltd

LONDON

I saw a
BEE

A book to share from
Scallywag Press

For Stan – the boy who saw the bee

First published in Great Britain in 2019
by Scallywag Press Ltd, 10 Sutherland Row, London SW1V 4JT
This paperback edition published 2020

Text and illustration copyright © Rob Ramsden, 2019

Printed on FSC paper in China by Toppan Leefung

001

British Library Cataloguing in Publication Data available
ISBN 978-1-912650-34-7

This is me.

I looked in a box.
I saw a bee!

The bee saw me!

I was scared.
I chased the bee . . .

The bee
chased me!

Buzzzzz!

I climbed
into the box
and I hid
from the bee.

And then,
guess what?

It hid from me.

I looked for the bee,

this way . . .

. . . and that.

No bee!

No bee.

No bee . . .

I missed the bee.
Did the bee miss me?

I listened.
I heard . . .

BUZZ   BUZZZ

I followed
the sound . . .

Buzz Buzzz Buzzzzzz

Buuzzzzzz   Buuzzzzzzzzzzzzzzz

We both buzzed around...

and around

and around...

and around

Buzz   Buzzz!

I had found the bee!

The bee had found me . . .

I love the bee.
The bee loves me.